Dear Parent:

Congratulations! Your child is taking
the first steps on an exciting journey.
The destination? Independent reading!

STEP INTO READING® will help your child get there. The program offers
five steps to reading success. Each step includes fun stories and colorful art.
There are also Step into Reading Sticker Books, Step into Reading Math
Readers, Step into Reading Write-In Readers, Step into Reading Phonics
Readers, and Step into Reading Phonics First Steps! Boxed Sets—a complete
literacy program with something for every child.

Learning to Read, Step by Step!

Ready to Read Preschool–Kindergarten
• big type and easy words • rhyme and rhythm • picture clues
For children who know the alphabet and are eager to
begin reading.

Reading with Help   Preschool–Grade 1
• basic vocabulary • short sentences • simple stories
For children who recognize familiar words and sound out
new words with help.

Reading on Your Own Grades 1–3
• engaging characters • easy-to-follow plots • popular topics
For children who are ready to read on their own.

Reading Paragraphs Grades 2–3
• challenging vocabulary • short paragraphs • exciting stories
For newly independent readers who read simple sentences
with confidence.

Ready for Chapters Grades 2–4
• chapters • longer paragraphs • full-color art
For children who want to take the plunge into chapter books
but still like colorful pictures.

STEP INTO READING® is designed to give every child a successful
reading experience. The grade levels are only guides. Children can progress
through the steps at their own speed, developing confidence in their
reading, no matter what their grade.

Remember, a lifetime love of reading starts with a single step!

Special thanks to Vicki Jaeger, Monica Okazaki, Kathleen Warner, Emily Kelly, Christine Chang, Tanya Mann, Rob Hudnut, Tiffany J. Shuttleworth, Walter P. Martishius, Luke Carroll, Lil Reichmann, Pam Prostarr, David Lee, Anita Lee, Andrea Schimpl, Tulin Ulkutay, and Ayse Ulkutay

Visit us on the Web!
www.stepintoreading.com
www.randomhouse.com/kids
www.barbie.com

Educators and librarians, for a variety of teaching tools, visit us at
www.randomhouse.com/teachers

Library of Congress Control Number: 2009935386
ISBN: 978-0-375-86450-6 (trade) — 978-0-375-96450-3 (lib. bdg)

Printed in the United States of America
10 9 8

Barbie
in
A Mermaid Tale

Adapted by Christy Webster
Based on the original screenplay by Elise Allen
Illustrated by Ulkutay Design Group
and Pat Pakula

Random House 🏠 New York

Merliah loves to surf.
She is the best surfer
in Malibu.

Merliah's hair turns
pink!
She dives
underwater.
She can breathe!

Merliah meets Zuma.

Zuma is a dolphin.

Zuma talks!

Zuma tells Merliah
about her past.
Merliah is half
mermaid!

Merliah's mother was
a mermaid named
Calissa.
Merliah's mother
gave her a necklace.

Merliah does not
believe Zuma.
She smashes
the necklace.

Mermaid magic
comes out.
It shows them
Merliah's mother.
She is in trouble.

"Please help her,"
Zuma says.

Merliah agrees.

They swim deep
into the ocean.

Merliah and Zuma
go to Oceana.
It is a pretty city
underwater.

Calissa is the true
queen of Oceana.
But Merliah's evil
aunt Eris is now queen.
She keeps Calissa
in prison.

Two mermaids
give Merliah
a fake tail.

They will help Merliah.

So will Snouts.

He is a baby sea lion.

Merliah goes
to the Destinies.
They tell fortunes.

They tell her
to do three tasks.
Then she can beat Eris.

Merliah climbs high.
She does
the first task.

She finds
the magic comb!

Now Merliah must
find a dreamfish.
Zuma knows where to go.

Eris's manta sharks
chase them.
They must escape!

Merliah surfs
a huge current.
She meets
a dreamfish!

The dreamfish
loves Merliah's surfing.
He will help her.

Merliah has
one more task.
She needs Eris's
necklace.

Merliah has a plan.

She grabs the necklace!

Eris is angry.

Eris traps Merliah in a whirlpool.

Merliah accepts that
she is a mermaid.
She gets a real
mermaid tail!

Merliah escapes!
Eris is trapped
in the whirlpool
instead.
Oceana is saved!

Calissa is free!
Merliah finally
meets her mother.
Calissa gives Merliah
a new magic necklace.
Merliah has a home
in both worlds!